The Not-So-Tiny Tales of

SIMON SEAHORSE

Seas the Day!

By Cora Reef
Illustrated by Jake McDonald

LITTLE SIMON

New York London Toronto Sydney New Delhi

LITTLE SIMON
An imprint of Simon & Schuster Children's Publishing Division
1230 Avenue of the Americas, New York, New York 10020
First Little Simon paperback edition July 2023
Copyright © 2023 by Simon & Schuster, Inc. Also available in a Little Simon hardcover edition. All rights reserved, including the right of reproduction in whole or in part in any form. LITTLE SIMON is a registered trademark of Simon & Schuster, Inc., and associated colophon is a trademark of Simon & Schuster, Inc. For information about special discounts for bulk purchases, please contact Simon & Schuster Special Sales at 1-866-506-1949 or business@simonandschuster.com. The Simon & Schuster Speakers Bureau can bring authors to your live event. For more information or to book an event contact the Simon & Schuster Speakers Bureau at 1-866-248-3049 or visit our website at www.simonspeakers.com. Designed by Leslie Mechanic. The text of this book was set in Causten Round. Manufactured in the United States of America 0623 LAK
10 9 8 7 6 5 4 3 2 1
Library of Congress Cataloging-in-Publication Data. Names: Reef, Cora, author. | McDonald, Jake, illustrator. Title: Seas the day! / Cora Reef ; illustrated by Jake McDonald. Description: First Little Simon paperback edition. | New York : Little Simon, 2023. | Series: The not-so-tiny tales of Simon Seahorse ; 8 | Audience: Ages 5-9 | Audience: Grades K-1 | Summary: Simon learns his friend DeeDee is moving away from Coral Grove, and knows he will miss his friend, so he plans the best day ever, even if some have doubts. Identifiers: LCCN 2022042903 (print) | LCCN 2022042904 (ebook) | ISBN 9781665929677 (paperback) | ISBN 9781665929684 (hardcover) | ISBN 9781665929691 (ebook) Subjects: CYAC: Sea horses–Fiction. | Marine life–Fiction. | Friendship–Fiction. | LCGFT: Picture books. Classification: LCC PZ7.1.R4423 Se 2023 (print) | LCC PZ7.1.R4423 (ebook) | DDC [Fic]–dc23. LC record available at https://lccn.loc.gov/2022042903. LC ebook record available at https://lccn.loc.gov/2022042904

Contents

DeeDee's
News

"And then Orion zoomed past the sea snake so fast that it accidentally tied itself in a knot! After that we sped away from Wave Beach," Simon Seahorse said.

His best friend, Olive Octopus, laughed. "So . . . how much of that story *really* happened?" she asked as she and Simon swam toward school.

"Well . . . ," Simon began.

Just then, Cam Crab scuttled by. "Knowing Simon and his stories," Cam said, "probably *none* of it."

Simon smiled. Cam's crabbiness didn't bother him.

"Well," said Simon, "my brother Orion and I *did* go to Wave Beach this weekend. The rest might not have happened *exactly* like I said. But it's fun to imagine, isn't it?" There was nothing Simon liked more than a good story.

"I guess so," Cam said, shuffling away.

Olive smiled. "It *is* fun to imagine. But I think your imagination might be a little bigger than ours, Simon."

Finally Simon and Olive reached Coral Grove Elementary. They swam up the reef to Ms. Tuttle's classroom.

Simon settled into his seat next to his friend DeeDee. "I like your shell necklace!" he told her.

"Thanks!" said DeeDee. "I made it all by myself."

"Do you think you could show me how to do it?" Simon asked.

A strange look passed over DeeDee's face. "Oh, I don't know," she said slowly.

Just then Ms. Tuttle called out, "Good morning, class! Today we'll be talking about the importance of phytoplankton. Did you know that it's a food source for everything from zooplankton to whales?"

Simon sat up straight, forgetting about DeeDee's necklace. He loved learning about the different creatures in the ocean. You never knew when you'd meet a new one!

After the class did some worksheets—and Simon did some daydreaming about whales—it was time for recess. But instead of sending everyone out to the playground, Ms. Tuttle called DeeDee up to the front of the room.

"DeeDee has some news to share with us," Ms. Tuttle explained.

"I wanted to let everyone know that my family and I are moving out of Coral Grove!" DeeDee said, bouncing with excitement.

Everyone around Simon gasped. Some friends clapped. But Simon only stared at DeeDee, not sure how to feel. This must be why DeeDee had acted so strangely when Simon asked

her about making shell necklaces.
She wouldn't be in town long enough
to show him how!

But why would anyone ever leave
Coral Grove?

The Perfect Idea

At recess everyone crowded around DeeDee on the playground.

"Where is your family going?" asked Lionel.

"We're moving to Tidal Isle to be closer to my baby cousins," DeeDee explained. "They're so cute. I'm excited to see them all the time!"

"Tidal Isle," Cam repeated with a frown. "Never heard of it."

"Oh, it's amazing!" DeeDee said. "The streets are lined with golden sea grass, and all the homes are decorated with tropical sea fans.

Plus, there's a whirlpool fountain in the center of town that's supposed to make wishes come true."

Simon's mouth gaped open. Now he could see why someone could be excited to move. Tidal Isle sounded pretty fantastic!

"When do you leave?" Olive asked.

"This Sunday," DeeDee said. "My room is already packed up."

"Wow, that's really soon," said Lionel.

DeeDee's smile faded. "I'm excited about our new home, but it'll be hard to say goodbye to Coral Grove," she admitted.

"We're really going to miss you," said Nix, her long eel tail drooping.

The others nodded. Suddenly nobody seemed excited anymore.

Simon couldn't believe that DeeDee would be leaving Coral Grove forever!

He should give her something to remember her old home by. But how could he possibly put everything great about Coral Grove in one place?

Then Simon had the *perfect* idea.

"DeeDee," he said suddenly. "Before you go, we're going to throw you the best last day in Coral Grove *ever!*"

Olive turned to look at Simon. "We are?" she asked.

"Yes!" Simon cried. "Just you wait, DeeDee. I can't tell you anything about it because it's going to be a surprise. But I *can* tell you that we are going to *seas* the day!"

"Wow! Thank you, Simon," said DeeDee. "That sounds great!"

As everyone scattered across the playground, Olive gave Simon a nudge with her arm. "What kind of tricks do you have up your fins this time?" she asked.

Simon smiled. "Nothing yet," he admitted. "But I will! Let's meet here after school so we can start planning for Saturday."

"But that's the day after tomorrow! Are you sure we have enough time to put together a big surprise by then?" said Olive.

"Don't worry. We'll come up with something great," Simon assured her.

Then he jumped up and cried, "race you to the seashell swings!"

Simon took off, his fins flapping wildly—and his mind swirling with ideas for DeeDee's perfect last day in Coral Grove.

Here's the Plan!

At the end of the day, Simon and Olive said goodbye to their classmates. Simon started to swim away, but then hurried back to give DeeDee one last hug.

"Come on, Simon," Olive said as she gently pulled him away. "DeeDee isn't leaving town yet. You'll see her tomorrow!"

"I know, but if I give her plenty of hugs now, she'll have some extra stored up when she gets to Tidal Isle," Simon explained.

Olive laughed. "I guess that's true."

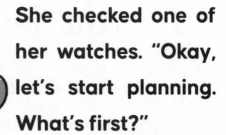

She checked one of her watches. "Okay, let's start planning. What's first?"

Simon took out the list he'd made during lunch. "First we go to Seagrass Fields," Simon read aloud. "Come on!"

They swam down the reef and hopped into the current that would take them across town.

"Why are we heading to Seagrass Fields?" Olive asked as they were whisked along. "Do you have bubble ball practice today?"

"Nope," said Simon. "I think DeeDee's last day should end with a performance, and Seagrass Fields is the perfect spot. But we need to check with Mr. Ray, the groundskeeper, to make sure it's okay."

"What sort of performance?" Olive asked, frowning. "We didn't have the easiest time learning a routine for the school showcase, remember?"

"I'm not sure yet," Simon admitted.

They hopped out of the current at Seagrass Fields, and Simon waved for Olive to follow him. "Mr. Ray's office is this way," he said.

They swam toward the coral stands on the far side of the field. Mr. Ray's office was tucked underneath.

"Simon!" Mr. Ray said. "I'm surprised to see you here on a non-practice day."

"I came to ask if we could use the field on Saturday afternoon," Simon explained. "We're planning a show as part of a surprise for our friend who's moving away."

"Let me check the schedule," Mr. Ray said. He hummed to himself as he looked through his sand-dollar calendar. "Hmm, we'll be mowing the seagrass on Saturday morning. But you're in luck! The afternoon is wide open!"

"So we can use the field?" Simon asked.

Mr. Ray nodded. "That's right. I'll put you on the schedule!"

Simon beamed. So far his plan was coming along perfectly. "Thanks, Mr. Ray! We'll see you on Saturday!"

"Where to now?" Olive asked as they headed back toward the current. "Our next stop is..." Simon checked his list again. "Whale Way."

Olive's eyes widened in surprise. "Why, what's there?"

"You'll see," Simon said with a little smile. "Come on!"

The Rest
of the Plan

As Simon and Olive swam through Whale Way, the water grew colder and colder. Up ahead, Simon spotted two enormous whales gliding past.

"We're almost there," he told Olive.

"*Now* can you tell me what we're doing here?" Olive asked, looking around nervously.

"We're visiting my friend Walter," Simon answered. "I want to ask him if he'll be our transportation for DeeDee's last day."

"Can't we just take the turtle trolley? Or ride the current?" said Olive.

Simon shook his head. "It'll be a lot easier if we all ride together on Walter's back. *And* a lot more fun!"

When they reached a cluster of large rocks, Simon stopped and called out, "Walter! Are you home?"

A moment later, a giant orca poked his head out from behind a curtain of seaweed. He was black and white with a bull's-eye circle by his eye.

"Oh, hi, Simon!" the whale said. "And Olive! It's nice to see you again!"

Olive gave him a nervous wave.

"Walter," said Simon, "we're planning a special going-away surprise on Saturday for our friend DeeDee, and we were wondering if you could give everyone a ride."

"Sure!" Walter said. "Sounds fun!"

"But *where* exactly will Walter be taking us?" asked Olive.

"To Red Reef Springs for bubble jumping!" cried Simon. "My dad used to go all the time when he was younger."

Olive frowned. "But *we've* never been there before. We don't even know what it's like."

"Exactly," said Simon. "And neither does DeeDee. Don't you think she should check it out before she leaves?"

"I . . . I guess so," said Olive, but she didn't sound very sure.

"Don't worry. DeeDee will love it." Simon turned back to Walter. "We'll see you on Saturday?"

"You bet!" said Walter.

As Simon and Olive headed back
to the current, the water was still
chilly. *"Brr,"* said Simon. "Let's go
warm up with some hot kelp milk at
the Barnacle Bakery."

"I thought you liked Sandy's
Candies better," said Olive.

"I do, but the Barnacle Bakery is
DeeDee's favorite. I heard her raving
about Chef Claude's kelp donuts."

Inside the bakery, they found Chef Claude icing a large kelp cake. When they told him about DeeDee moving away, he seemed disappointed. But he said he'd be happy to help.

"I can send over some kelp donuts to Seagrass Fields," Chef Claude offered. "That way you can end the day with a sweet treat."

"Thanks, Chef Claude!" said Simon.

As Simon and Olive left the bakery sipping their hot kelp milk, Simon checked his list again and smiled. Things for DeeDee's special last day were coming together perfectly!

The
Electric Eelies

The next morning at school, Simon made sure DeeDee was busy talking to Ms. Tuttle. Then he filled his other friends in on the plan for DeeDee's going-away surprise the next day.

"So we'll be riding a whale, going bubble jumping, *and* having kelp donuts?" asked Lionel. "That sounds like the perfect day to me!"

"Kelp donuts?" Cam grumbled. "I like Chef Claude's cinnamon kelp buns better."

"But this is a surprise for *DeeDee*, remember?" Olive said with a laugh.

Cam sighed. "I guess I can eat a donut if I *have* to."

"And after the donuts, we'll be ending the day with a show at Seagrass Fields," said Simon. "Now I just need to figure out what *kind* of show—and fast!"

Cam frowned. "We won't have to dance again, will we?"

"No," said Simon, shaking his head.
"There's not enough time to learn a
new routine, and everyone's already
seen our old one."

"Maybe we could ask someone else
to perform," Olive suggested.

"Maybe," said Simon. "But *who*?"

Everyone thought for a moment.

Then Nix's tail lit up. "I have an idea!" she said. "Do you know the Electric Eelies?"

"The ribbon-eel dance group?" asked Simon.

"Yes. DeeDee loves them!" said Nix. "My cousin is a member of the group. I can ask him if they'd want to perform."

"That would be great!" said Simon.

"All right, let's all meet at Whale Way after lunch tomorrow."

Everyone nodded and then swam off to their desks. Simon wiggled with excitement as he imagined the look on DeeDee's face when she saw the Electric Eelies performing just for her!

"Simon," Olive whispered as they took their seats. "I had another idea for a surprise for DeeDee."

"What is it?" Simon whispered back. He glanced to make sure DeeDee was still distracted.

"What if I put together a collection of drawings and stories from DeeDee's friends as a going-away present?" said Olive. "That way she'll be able to take part of us with her."

"That's a great idea!" said Simon.

Just then, DeeDee swam over. "What's a great idea?" she asked.

Simon and Olive jumped apart, looking guilty.

"Oh, um. N-nothing, really...," Olive stammered.

"It's a surprise," Simon jumped in. "But we *can* tell you to meet us at Whale Way tomorrow after lunch."

DeeDee's eyes went wide. "Whale Way? Isn't that kind of far?"

"Trust me," Simon told her. "It will be worth the trip."

A Story
to Remember

That night, Simon was in a great mood. Nix had stopped by after dinner to tell him that the Electric Eelies had agreed to perform at Seagrass Fields the next afternoon. It would be the perfect way to end DeeDee's last day in Coral Grove.

Now, Simon just had to come up with something special for Olive's collection. He sat down at his desk, thinking. DeeDee liked sparkle almost as much as he did. Should he make

her a glitter sand picture? No, he was certain someone else would do that. More than anything, Simon wanted DeeDee to remember his stories.

So, Simon took out some paper and began to write.

Once there was a fish named DeeDee who had a magical gift. Whatever she touched with her fin turned glittery. As DeeDee swam through Coral Grove, she made the entire town sparkle.

But one day, a squid monster appeared.

"Roar!" roared the squid monster. "Coral Grove is too sparkly! I must destroy it!"

DeeDee tried to stop the monster, but her glitter only made it angrier.

Simon looked up from his paper. Hmm. Something didn't feel quite right. He wanted to write about DeeDee, but he *also* wanted to write about her friends.

He twirled his pencil with his fin as his mind swirled with ideas. Finally, Simon smiled and started scribbling again.

Just then, DeeDee's friends Simon, Olive, Cam, Lionel, and Nix arrived to help.

"I tried to stop the squid monster with my glitter, but it didn't work," DeeDee told them.

"I don't like glitter. It sticks to my claws," Cam grumbled.

"DeeDee, look!" said Olive. "Your glitter didn't stop the monster, but it did make it weaker."

"We'll distract the squid monster while you cover it in more sparkles," said Simon.

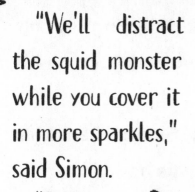

"Perfect idea!" said DeeDee.

The friends worked together, and soon the squid monster was covered in glitter. "Argh!" it roared.

Angry and with glitter all over, the monster fled Coral Grove and was never seen again.

Simon was just finishing up his story when there was a knock on his bedroom door.

"Are you still up, Simon?" said Mr. Seahorse, popping his head in.

Simon blinked in surprise. He hadn't realized how late it was. "Sorry, Dad. I was just working on a story for DeeDee. I want it to be just right."

"I'm sure she'll like whatever you come up with," Mr. Seahorse said.

"I know," said Simon. "But I want to give her something really special, so she doesn't forget me."

Mr. Seahorse chuckled. "Simon,"

he said, "I don't think anyone could forget *you*. Now hop into bed."

Simon drifted off to sleep, dreaming of giant squids and electric eels and donuts.

7

Whale Waiting

The next afternoon, Simon met Olive at the corner of Seaweed Lane like he did almost every day. But this time, the pair didn't head to school. Instead, they took the current to Whale Way to join their friends.

"Here's my gift for DeeDee," said Simon.

"Thanks! I'll add it to my collection."
Olive tried to take the story from
Simon, but his tail was still wrapped
around it. "Uh, Simon? Are you okay?"

"Oh, sorry," he said, letting go of the paper. "I guess I'm a little nervous about today."

"Don't worry. Everything will go just fine," Olive assured him.

As they hopped out of the current at Whale Way, they had to leap out of the path of a humpback whale.

"Wow, it's busy here today," Olive said as more whales whooshed past.

"It's hard to see where we're going."

Oops. Simon realized that he'd forgotten to warn his friends about how crowded Whale Way could get on the weekend. But it was too late now.

Simon and Olive waited by the current. Soon, Cam hopped out—the first to arrive. To Simon's surprise, Cam actually looked excited.

"I've never ridden a whale before, or gone bubble jumping," Cam said. "Where is Walter, anyway?"

"He should be here soon," said Simon, scanning the stream of whales passing by.

A few moments later, Lionel arrived. "Nix will meet us later at Seagrass Fields," he explained. "She'll bring the Electric Eelies with her."

Simon looked around again, but there was still no sign of Walter—or DeeDee.

"Walter *is* real, right?" asked Cam. "He's not just one of your stories?"

"Of course he's real," said Simon. But now he was growing even more nervous. Why wasn't Walter there yet? And where was DeeDee? He *had* told them the right day, hadn't he?

Just when Simon was starting to get really worried, he spotted Walter heading toward them. And riding on his back ... was DeeDee!

"Sorry we're late!" Walter called out, coming to a stop. "I had to give my new friend here a ride."

DeeDee looked embarrassed as she slid off Walter's back. "I got a little lost in the crowd," she explained. "I was about to give up and head home when Walter found me."

"I didn't want DeeDee to miss her own party!" Walter said with a laugh.

"I'm sorry, DeeDee!" Simon cried. "We should have come here together. Then you wouldn't have gotten lost."

"It's all right," DeeDee said brightly.
"I'm here now."

Everyone turned to look at Simon.
He realized they were waiting for him
to tell them where to go next.

He took a deep breath. "All right," he called out. "Let's all hop on Walter's back and head to our first stop!"

To Bubble Jump or Not to Bubble Jump?

As the group swam toward Red Reef Springs, Walter made the ride as fun as possible. He did loop the loops and dips and spins. Everyone was having a great time.

Everyone except DeeDee.

"Are you all right?" Simon asked, noticing she'd gone from her usual bluish color to more of a green.

"I'm just feeling a bit seasick," DeeDee said weakly.

Oh no. "Walter!" Simon called out. "Can you slow down?"

As soon as Walter stopped doing tricks, DeeDee started to look better. But now Simon felt bad. The ride was supposed to be fun for DeeDee—not make her sick!

Finally, they arrived at Red Reef Springs. Everyone hopped off Walter's back and swam to the edge. They looked down.

And down.

And down.

"Wow," said Lionel. "This is really . . .

high."

Simon gulped as he watched some older sea creatures jump from the top of the cliff onto the bubbles below. Red Reef Springs was a lot bigger than he'd imagined.

Still, they'd come all this way. And maybe the drop wasn't as bad as it looked.

Simon took a deep breath. "So," he said, trying to keep his voice from shaking, "who's ready for bubble jumping?"

Everyone looked at him, but no one answered.

"Are we sure it's safe?" Olive finally asked.

"Of course," said Simon. "My dad used to bubble jump here all the time."

"Are you sure we're old enough?" asked Cam.

"I...I don't know," Simon admitted. He realized that Mr. Seahorse hadn't said how old he and his friends had been when they visited.

"What if . . . ," DeeDee said in a soft voice, "we save bubble jumping for when I come back to visit Coral Grove?"

"That's a great idea," Lionel said quickly, and everyone else agreed.

Simon's tail sagged. Red Reef Springs *was* a little scarier than he expected, but he was still disappointed that no one wanted to do the first part of his plan.

"I'm glad we got to see this place, though," DeeDee said. "It's really pretty here."

Simon looked around and realized she was right. He'd been so busy thinking about his plan, he hadn't even noticed how colorful it was.

And this *was* only the *first* part of the plan, Simon reminded himself. There was still plenty of fun to be had! Since they'd gotten to Red Reef Springs late, they'd be perfectly on time for the second part of their adventure.

"All right, everyone," Simon called out. "Next stop: Seagrass Fields!"

The
Final Act

When they got to Seagrass Fields, everyone hopped off Walter's back.

"Thanks for the ride!" said Simon.

"Happy to help," Walter said. Then he turned and glided away.

Simon waved for his friends to follow him. But when they got down to the actual field, Simon stared in shock.

The field was covered in sea cows!

"I thought no one was using the field this afternoon," said Olive.

Simon spotted Mr. Ray nearby. "Wasn't the mowing supposed to be this morning?" Simon asked him.

"Sorry," Mr. Ray said. "The grounds crew got a late start. If you don't mind waiting, they should be done soon."

"But the Electric Eelies will be here any minute!" said Simon.

Suddenly, he spotted Nix swimming toward him with a frown on her face.

"Nix, what's wrong?" asked Simon.

"I have some bad news," she said. "The Eelies forgot they already agreed to perform at a birthday party in Seal Cove today. They won't have time to make it here, too."

Simon's heart sank. "You mean they're *not coming*?"

Nix shook her head. "I'm sorry, Simon," she said.

"It's not your fault," Simon reassured her.

But he couldn't believe it. The show had been the best part of his plan, and now it wasn't even going to happen!

"What's wrong?" DeeDee asked as she and the others swam over.

Simon opened his mouth to explain, but he was too upset to speak.

"Simon had a really great last day planned for you," Nix told DeeDee. "Including a performance by the Electric Eelies."

"We know they're your favorite ribbon-eel dance group," said Lionel.

DeeDee's eyes widened. "Wow. That *does* sound great."

"But it turns out the Eelies can't make it today," said Nix.

"Bummer," said Cam.

Simon slumped onto the coral stands. After all his planning, DeeDee's perfect last day had turned into a perfect *Dee-saster*.

"I'm sorry, DeeDee," he said. "I guess we should give up and head home."

Just then, someone called out, "Is this the going-away party?"

Simon turned to see Chef Claude at the edge of the field. He was holding a tray full of pastries.

With everything going on, Simon had forgotten all about *this* part of the plan!

"Are those kelp donuts?" cried DeeDee. "They're my favorite!"

"What do you think, Simon?" asked Olive. "Maybe we can all have a donut before we go?"

Simon didn't feel like eating, but he could tell all his friends were excited about the treats. "I guess we can't let the donuts go to waste," he said.

The others cheered and hurried over to Chef Claude. Soon the whole gang was enjoying the donuts. Even Simon managed to nibble on one. It was delicious.

Simon sighed. At least one small part of his plan had gone right.

Perfectly Almost Perfect

"Simon, look!" said DeeDee as everyone finished up their kelp donuts. "The sea cows are done mowing the field!"

"But the Eelies aren't coming, remember?" Simon said.

"No," said DeeDee, "but since we're already here, why don't we play some bubble ball?"

The others nodded, and even Cam seemed to like the idea.

"Well, all right," said Simon. "Come on. I know where Mr. Ray keeps extra equipment."

After everyone got ready, they broke up into two teams. Then they started to play. The grounds crew stayed to watch from the stands.

The game wasn't like the matches Simon played with his bubble ball team. Olive kept popping the ball, and Lionel kept swimming the wrong way. But even though it wasn't a "real" match, it was still a great game. And the sea cows' cheers for both teams made it even better.

Simon was having so much fun, he forgot all about his failed plan. At the end of the match, everyone helped themselves to more kelp donuts.

"Thank you for putting together such a great last day for me, Simon," said DeeDee.

"I just wish things had gone better," he told her. "I wanted your last day in Coral Grove to be one you'd remember forever."

DeeDee laughed. "Are you kidding? I *almost* got sick riding a whale, *almost* jumped off a cliff, and *almost* saw the Electric Eelies. How could I *ever* forget all that?"

Simon smiled. The day certainly had been an adventure!

"Besides," DeeDee went on, "what could be better than spending my last day in Coral Grove with my friends?"

"DeeDee," Olive said, swimming over. "We made you something." She held out a glass bottle full of colorful pieces of paper. "They're pictures and stories for you to remember us by."

DeeDee's face lit up. "Wow, thank you! I have something for each of you, too." She passed out sparkly seashell necklaces to everyone.

Simon blinked back happy tears as he put on his necklace. Then he gave DeeDee one last hug.

It was the perfect ending to a not-so-perfect day.

A few weeks later, Simon spotted Miss Abby dropping something in his mailbox.

"Thanks, Miss Abby!" Simon called as the mail carrier slowly made her way down the road.

Simon pulled open the mailbox to
find a postcard. It was from DeeDee!

GREETING FROM TIDAL ISLE!

On the front was an amazing picture of a whirlpool fountain. Underneath were the words: GREETINGS FROM TIDAL ISLE!

Simon turned the postcard over, and there was a note from DeeDee!

Hi, Simon!
Things in Tidal Isle are
going great! I miss my
Coral Grove friends, but
your stories and pictures
almost make it feel like
you're all here with me.
Yesterday I made a wish
in the whirlpool fountain
that you would come
visit. I hope my wish
comes true soon!
From,
DeeDee

Simon read the postcard and smiled. Visit Tidal Isle? That sounded like a great way to see DeeDee again— *and* to gather lots of new ideas for his stories!

SIMON'S STORY

Sara Seahorse was super excited to visit her best friend, Dixie, in Tidal Isle. Sara had never been before, but Dixie had always talked about the wishing fountain at the center of town. Sara had already made a list of wishes. With her suitcase packed and best hat on, Sara took the long current ride. Dixie was waiting when she arrived in Tidal Isle. And their first stop was the fountain! Dixie explained that in order for your wish to come true, as you threw your sand dollar in, you had to think of

something you really wanted. Sara closed her eyes and thought about what she'd written on her list. More than anything, she always wanted to have ideas for her stories.
In her head, she made this wish and threw a sand dollar into the fountain. When she opened her eyes, she immediately grabbed her notebook and sea pen and started writing. She had so many ideas! Dixie smiled and put an arm around Sara. She was very glad to have her friend there.

THE END

Here's a peek at Simon's next big adventure!

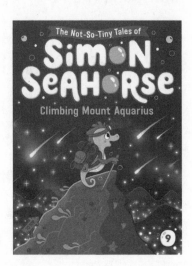

It was dinnertime at the Seahorse house, but everyone was so focused on the story being told that they'd barely touched their kelp spaghetti.

"Sir Sheldon knew that if he didn't make it to the top of Mount Aquarius

An excerpt from *Climbing Mount Aquarius*

by that evening, it would be too dark to continue."

"And then he'd have to go home?" Simon Seahorse asked, his voice hushed.

Simon's dad nodded.

Usually, *Simon* was the one who shared exciting tales with his eleven brothers and sisters during mealtimes. But tonight, it was Mr. Seahorse's turn.

"Sir Sheldon decided that he had come too far to turn back," Mr. Seahorse went on. "As he neared the top of the mountain, it grew so dark that he could barely see his own claws!

An excerpt from *Climbing Mount Aquarius*

"But suddenly, a magical glow lit his path. He spied a handwritten sign that said TO TOP and he decided to trust whoever had made that sign, even though the little path wasn't on the map he was using. Well, it was a good thing he did, because Sir Sheldon scrambled the rest of the way to the summit. He'd done it! He'd reached the top of Mount Aquarius!"

Everyone cheered as Mr. Seahorse took a bow. Then, finally, they dug into their spaghetti, chatting excitedly.

An excerpt from *Climbing Mount Aquarius*